W9-ACF-306

Soup on Ice

ROBERT NEWTON PECK

Soup on Ice

Illustrated by Charles Robinson

A Yearling Book

Published by
Dell Publishing
a division of
The Bantam Doubleday Dell Publishing Group, Inc.
666 Fifth Avenue
New York, New York 10103

ISBN: 0-440-40115-1

Reprinted by arrangement with Alfred A. Knopf, Inc.

Printed in the United States of America

December 1988

10   9   8   7   6   5

CW

Soup on Ice

1

"It's too cold to go to school," said Soup.

My pal Soup stood in our kitchen, near the big black cookstove that said Acme American on its iron flank. Heavy snow from his boots was rapidly becoming twin puddles of gray slush on Mama's hardwood floor.

My mother looked at Soup. "Luther Vinson, you and Robert are *both* going to school this morning, and that's all there is to it."

"Okay," I sighed. "I'm most ready."

"Wait," said Mama. "One more sweater, Rob."

"No," I told her, "I don't need it. Because I already got on two sets of long underwear. I'm wearing so much stuff that I'm three times my normal size."

"Robert, don't argue," Aunt Carrie commanded in a resolute voice. "You know that it's *winter*."

I knew.

As I kicked and struggled, Aunt Carrie held me in a hammerlock, while Mama was thrusting me into my sweater, adding mittens, a six-foot scarf, a ten-pound coat, and topped off by a scratchy woolen hat that, in keeping with her idea of fashion, she tugged down to my upper lip.

Squinting through the fuzzy fibers of my facial fortification, I noticed that Soup was also robed, wrapped, laced, buckled, and bundled to three times *his* normal size.

Why? Because it was December.

Every winter, there are only *two* locales in the entire Northern Hemisphere that compete for the honor of being the coldest spot on Earth for the longest time. One is the North Pole. The other is Learning, Vermont, where the polar wind whistles crisply down Lake Champlain in search of helpless prey.

In such weather, only *one* of God's creatures dares to set foot out-of-doors. All others stay inside. Horses, cows, pigs, dogs, cats, sheep, geese, ducks, chickens, and grown-up people cozily remain in barns, sheds, houses, coops, and stables.

Kids, however, are sent to school.

"Off you go," ordered Mama.

Bracing themselves, Mama and Aunt Carrie heaved their farm-hardened Yankee shoulders to our storm door. Aunt Carrie propped it open for one full second, long enough for Mama to propel Soup and me outside to our frozen fate beneath a pewter sky.

Bang!

The storm door slammed closed behind us, our only heated haven denied, our one hope now being either to make it to school or die.

"We better run," said Soup. "Come on, Rob."

We ran.

Into a merciless wind we staggered, stumbled, fell; then heroically rose to battle onward, each of us leaning horizontally forward, like twin mermaids on the bowsprits of whaling ships. Soup Vinson and Robert Peck surged across the icy wasteland of frozen Vermont tundra, stabbing our respiratory systems with every inhalation of iron-clad ozone. Gray plumes of heavy breathing exhaled from our lungs and froze instantly in midair.

"Maybe," I yelled to Soup as we trotted to delay death, "we oughta go back home."

"Are you joking?" Soup hollered. "Nobody would crack open a door to let us in. Neither your folks nor mine."

Inch after inch we plodded. I felt relatively nothing, except misery, below my ankles or beyond my wrists.

"Well," Soup screamed through the howling wind, "I suppose we're lucky, Rob."

"Lucky?"

"Yup," he said. "Folks claim that December is a heat wave compared to January."

Had I still been fully alive, I would have laughed. Or at least faked it. Because, cold though it was, it felt warming to have me a pal like Soup. His real name was Luther Wesley Vinson. He was a year and four months older than I was, which meant that I eventually inherited most of his outgrowed clothes. Right now, I could have used every extra thread and wisp of lint.

As my nose was running, I sniffed.

"Cheer up, Rob," said Soup. "Christmas is coming."

The merry thought of Christmas lifted my feelings up to almost zero. It always did. For me, Christmas was redder than a ripe apple, even though it heralded the beginning of another whipping winter.

"Soon," said Soup, "we'll have to earn ourselves some money shoveling snow, so we can afford to buy presents for people."

"Right," I said, as we trudged along in our whitewashed world of winter.

"This year," Soup announced, "I'm giving Pa a plastic skull-head handle for the gearstick of his pickup truck. What are you going to buy for *your* pa?"

"I got it all planned," I told Soup. "I'm getting Papa a rattrap for the barn. It sort of looks like a mousetrap, only bigger. I'll give Aunt Carrie a bottle of laxative pills, to improve her temper. As for Mama, I'm buying her a a box of—a box of—" I sneezed.

"A box of candy?" Soup asked.

"No . . . mothballs. For the closet. What are you giving *your* mother?"

Soup chuckled. "I reckon I'll give Ma a pair of genuine Shirley Temple metal tap-dancing plates for her shoes."

I was hoping that somebody would give *me* earmuffs or Prestone.

As we final made it into the town of Learning, both of us automatically stopped to peek into Harry's Hardware Store. Beyond the frost-etched glass lay countless goodies to tempt even the most wary of Christmas shoppers. With our mittens cupping our eyes, Soup and I pressed our noses to the window to pay a silent tribute to one particular item.

There it was!

It was an Official Buck Jones Daisy Repeater BB Gun. Both of us sighed in devout worship.

"Wow!" I said.

"Thank gosh it's still there," said Soup.

"The last one," I whispered with reverence.

Because of our almost daily inquirings, we had learned from Mr. Harry Hoblicker, the proprietor, that a shipment of five Buck Jones BB Guns had arrived. Four had already been purchased. The gun in the window was the sole survivor of the shopping massacre. And now, before it became too late, it was time for each of us to redouble our hints at home.

For the past several days, I had printed reminders to Santa, with red crayon and in giant letters, asking, begging, pleading for only one Christmas present. Soup, at his house, had performed in a like manner. Our notes to Santa Claus, however, were never mailed at the Learning Post Office. No stamp was ever required. Instead, our repeated messages were intentionally "lost" in places where the adult members of our households would find them and then would yield (we hoped) to our fervent implorings.

For the past eight or nine nights, my nightmares featured a frantic foot race between two overweight shoppers, my mother and Soup's, both panting and puffing toward the finish line at Harry's Hardware, with eager arms outstretched to snare the prize—the very last Official Buck Jones Daisy Repeater BB Gun—for her deserving boy.

During my ardent campaign at home, I had committed only one tactical blunder. I'd expressed my one desire when Aunt Carrie happened to be within earshot. My stupidity only produced a long lecture on the limitless dangers of BB guns and the mindless parents who foolishly place such self-mutilating weaponry in the hands of innocent children.

"What a beauty," Soup sighed as his mitten wiped a cloud of breath from the window glass.

"If I don't get that BB gun," I said, "Christmas isn't going to be very merry for me."

Then the two of us tore ourselves away from Harry's Hardware Store and Christmas longings and headed listlessly for school.

"Look," said Soup, "the lake's icing over."

Sure enough, the deep autumn blue of Lake Champlain had hardened into a long gray mirror of solid ice.

"Maybe," I said, "we'll be able to go skating, come Saturday, if the ice is thick."

"Here in Vermont," said Soup, "when ice isn't yet quite thick enough, all you have to do is wait ten minutes. Hey, let's take ourselves one slide down the Double Zoomer."

"Okay."

What we called the Double Zoomer was the fastest ice slide in town. Two long and slender paths of ice, like a railroad track, already polished slick by many sliding young feet, stretched side by side and about a yard apart. Beneath the two narrow strips of ice, but now buried for the next five wintry months, lay a sidewalk, used in summertime for a stroll from our village square down the hill to the lake's edge.

With a running start, my feet went sliding on one track, Soup's on the other. We slid all the way to the bottom, a distance of about seventy feet, and coasted to a stop on the lake ice.

"Wow!" said Soup. "That ice is faster than a loose goose."

"Let's take another slide," I told him.

But we never got the chance. Because as we looked up the Double Zoomer somebody else was coming down, legs apart, with a foot on each ice path, and holding two gigantic chunks of snow.

"Oh, *no*," I said weakly, "it's Janice!"

"Run," said Soup.

We couldn't. The ice where Soup and I stood was too new and too slippery. My feet, also newly frozen inside boots and three pairs of woolen socks, just wouldn't respond. Whether it was fear or frost, I didn't know. Or care. All I saw was Janice Riker, the meanest and toughest kid in town. She was growing bigger, sliding faster, coming closer, closer, closer. . . .

Wham! Bam!

Getting hit in the chest with a big chunk of snow was painful enough. But after the cannonball came the cannon herself. Janice. A garbage truck would have been far more merciful.

My entire world turned white, purple, gold, black, and blue. Stars exploded. Comets erupted into countless sparks of agony. All I knew was that I was upside down, somewhere between Vermont and Siberia. Spinning through the air, I learned, was rather comfortable compared to landing on an icy lake.

Whack!

Soup landed. *Whump!* But he landed on top of *me,* which, I suppose, lessened his torment but didn't do too much to ease mine.

Opening my eyes, I looked up to see Janice Riker standing over us, doing a very rare thing. She was actual smiling, with all of the charm that her unbrushed fangs could offer.

"Merry Christmas, guys," said Janice.

2

"Egypt," said Miss Kelly.

Our teacher was standing at a large map of some place that she had pinned up against a wall, near the stove.

"Perhaps," said Miss Kelly, "the Three Wise Men came from Egypt, riding their camels, on that first Christmas Eve."

Using her long pointer, Miss Kelly touched a location on the map that I could have sworn was South America. I yawned. Geography wasn't my favorite subject. I looked at Norma Jean Bissell, who was.

"Centuries ago," said Miss Kelly, "the land of

Egypt was ruled by the pharaohs. And yesterday, we all learned that *pharaoh* is the name of a—"

"Poker game," said Janice.

Next to me, Soup snickered. But he didn't do it out loud. Nobody in his right mind would laugh at Janice Riker, even if he thought Janice's right mind was wrong. Behind me, I heard the familiar snarl of Eddy Tacker's rasping voice.

"No, it ain't," Eddy mumbled.

Up front, I saw Miss Kelly stand an inch taller and stiffen her crowbar spine. "Edward," she said, "if you have a contribution to make, please recite it to the entire class."

"Okay," said Eddy. "Because everybody knows. A pharaoh is a litter of pigs."

I knew that Janice and Eddy could often be as wrong as sin, and a nudge from Soup's elbow told me that maybe he thought so too.

"Well," said Miss Kelly, "in a certain sense, *both* of you are correct." She chalked the three words on our blackboard. "*Faro* is a card game. And a *farrow* is a pig litter."

"It is?" a kid asked her.

Miss Kelly smiled. "Indeed. The pharaoh in Egypt, however, was an ancient king, a ruler who lived thousands of—" Miss Kelly paused to listen.

Jingle! Jangle! Jingle!

"Whoa! And a ho-ho-ho!" a voice merrily yelled from outside our schoolhouse.

For certain, I recognized the sound. Sleigh bells!

14

Yet I knew better than to leave my bench and go racing to the window, an impetuous act that Miss Kelly's hardwood ruler would not condone. Miss Kelly, however, did go to the window, to look outside and then smile. She turned back to us.

"Class," she said, "we have a visitor."

We all hooted. Anything that would disrupt the pangs of Egypt and the rest of South America was, in my mind, a blessing.

"But," our teacher warned us in a quiet voice, "we shall all exhibit our *company manners.*"

"Yes'm," most of us said.

After a moment or two, the heavy door of our one-room school burst open, and in she came, stomping snow off her boots and jingling her strands of sleigh bells. The wind came, too, blowing arithmetic papers and scattering pages of homework into one unruly mess. Our visitor also carried a brown paper bag.

"Howdy!" howled Miss Boland.

With the thrust of her burly arm, she closed the door, turned, and faced Miss Kelly, who was one of her closest lifelong friends. Once inside, Miss Boland pulled off her mittens, loosened her giant winter coat, and hung it on a peg.

Miss Boland was our county nurse.

She was in charge of everybody's health; and some people claimed that, because of her tremendous dimensions, she shouldn't have been just a nurse. Miss Boland was more the size of a hospital.

Her totally white outfit appeared to be more starch than fabric. When she walked across the floor of our little school, her uniform rustled like a litter of kittens beneath a mussed-up Sunday newspaper.

I grinned.

When good old Miss Boland popped in at school, it usual meant exciting *news*. As it turned out, today was no exception to the custom.

"We're all set," Miss Boland proclaimed. "And it's really going to happen right here in Learning at the village square on Christmas Eve."

"Wonderful," said Miss Kelly. Turning to us, our teacher asked, "Class, would you like to hear about Miss Boland's surprise?"

"Yes'm," we responded.

All of us answered, I noticed, with the exception of Ally Tidwell. About a week ago, I'd been talking to Ally before school, and he told me that he didn't believe a whole lot in Christmas. It sounded sad the way he said it. But then he also said something nice. Ally hoped some of the little kids believed in Santa Claus.

Up front, Miss Boland was doing most of the talking, as she usual did, concerning her upcoming surprise.

"Well," said Miss Boland, warming her hands at the stove, then resting her white bulk in Miss Kelly's desk chair, "you've all seen the giant spruce tree downtown, in the village park."

We nodded.

"This year, on Christmas Eve, we're going to string lights on it, all colors, and we'll have the biggest and brightest Christmas tree in all Vermont."

Her announcement sure spread a grin on my face.

Soup was also smiling. But then he leaned closer to whisper in my ear. "I wonder what Miss Boland brought inside the paper bag."

It made me wonder too. And it also made me hope that Ally Tidwell would become a bit more enthusiastic about Christmas. Maybe, if we encouraged Ally a mite, he would.

"Now then," said Miss Boland with a dramatic wave of her white sleeve, "I s'pose all of you are curious about what's inside this little sack. So I'll tell you. Christmas presents! One for every girl and boy in the school."

We all cheered.

"Not so fast," Miss Kelly warned us. "Because, you see, Miss Boland and I have decided it's best that you receive your presents at our party, *after*—" She paused.

"Here it comes," said Soup.

"After all of you, next Monday, have handed in the themes that I assigned you to compose on the subject of 'What I Wish for Christmas.' Two pages long."

Silently I moaned. For me, writing a two-page composition was about as enjoyable as having my backside inoculated by a six-inch needle. And the agony lasted a whole lot longer. Yet I wondered what our presents were. As though she were reading my secret thoughts, Miss Boland held up her brown bag, and shook it.

Sure enough, *something* was inside.

Miss Kelly cleared her throat. "Yes, I realize that we're all excited because Christmas vacation is almost here. Still we shall persevere, as I expect you to do your very best on your compositions."

Taking the paper bag from Miss Boland, our teacher placed it in a bottom drawer of her desk, closed the drawer, and locked it with a key.

"Well," Miss Kelly asked us, "what do we always say when a friend like Miss Boland brings us a present for our upcoming school party?"

"Thank you," we dutifully chorused.

Miss Boland grinned. "You're all more than welcome, you kids." Rising from the chair, Miss Boland marched across the room, her unbuckled galoshes flapping like the wings of giant black bats. At the door she bundled herself into her heavy winter coat.

Miss Kelly thanked her again for coming.

"Oh," said Miss Boland, twisting around to look at us, "I near to forgot my other surprise. You youngsters are in for a special treat. And very soon."

In anticipation, I held my breath.

Miss Boland smiled. "Because you're all going to

try your doggone hardest on writing a theme, here's the special surprise. Somebody important will be coming to town on Christmas Eve, to sing carols with us around the big, lighted-up tree."

"Who?" we asked.

"Well," teased Miss Boland as she jingled her sleigh bells again, "this particular visitor is a large gentleman who wears a bright red suit and only comes to town at Christmas time."

"Santa Claus," we hollered in glee, all of us, except for one single kid.

Ally Tidwell.

3

"I'll use this one," said Soup.

It was Saturday morning, and the two of us were standing on Miss Witherspoon's front porch, close to town.

"You work the other one," Soup added.

We had brought two snow shovels with us. But I noticed real quick that Soup intended to use the smaller shovel.

"How come?" I asked him.

"Because," said Soup, "you're good at shoveling, and I'm better at edging. Besides, you're the boss. And a boss always goes first to lead the way."

During the night, more snow had fallen, which to Soup and me meant one thing. We could earn ourselves some quick Christmas money by clearing sidewalks for people, especially old ladies like Miss Witherspoon.

Earlier, she had informed Soup and me that all she really needed was a narrow path, one that would enable her to go back and forth from her house to her mailbox, which stood half buried at the road.

"You go first," Soup suggested, "and I'll sort of follow along behind, to make sure our edges are even."

"Okay," I sighed.

The first load of snow didn't feel too heavy on my shovel. Neither did the second or third. But the fourth was heavier. The fifth and sixth were stubborn, and the seventh weighed near to half a ton. Pausing for breath, I looked back over my shoulder to see Soup sitting on the porch's top step.

"Rob, old top, you're going just great."

"But *you're* not going at all," I told Soup, noticing that he hadn't even rearranged one flake.

"You *really* can shovel snow, Uncle Barney."

As I was a bit confused, I looked at Soup. "Hey," I asked him, "how come you called me Uncle Barney instead of Rob?"

"Oh . . . sorry. It's the way you shovel. You sure do remind me of my Uncle Barney," said Soup. "Yup, you certain do. Uncle Barney was the champion snow shoveler in the entire state of Vermont."

"Honest?"

Soup nodded. "Throw another load. I wanna watch to see if your style is really champion form."

I tossed away more snow.

"Nope," said Soup. "You don't quite have Uncle Barney's smooth delivery. I reckon anybody could see why. It's the *grip* on a shovel that starts a boy up that famous path which'll lead to becoming a state

22

champion. Uncle Barney showed me his *secret*."

"What secret?" I asked Soup.

My pal slowly got up from his seat on Miss Witherspoon's porch, stretched, and then strolled my way. I wondered why he didn't bother to bring along his shovel.

"Rob," he said, "if I thought you'd be serious about training, I'd be willing to be your coach." Soup shook his head. "But you probable aren't interested in becoming a state champ like Uncle Barney. You'd have to lug home a big silver trophy and maybe get kissed by Norma Jean Bissell."

Kissed, by Norma Jean! The thought made me forget how cold I was. I suddenly felt stronger and taller.

"Not every kid can handle fame," Soup went on to say. "Besides, the secret of becoming a state champion is so doggone simple that you'd probable just laugh at it."

"No, I wouldn't," I told Soup. "Come on, what's your Uncle Barney's secret? I gotta know."

Hands on his hips, Soup looked at the snow in front of me. Then he grinned. "It's all in the grip."

"The *grip?*"

"Right. Keep your right hand on the top end of your shovel, but slide your left hand way down near the load."

"Like this?"

"Good. Now throw a load or two and notice how much faster you can shovel."

I threw a load of snow.

"One more," Soup told me. "But this time, haul your left hand about an inch closer."

Throwing another load, I asked, "Is this right?"

"Sort of. Your grip looks a mite improved. The trouble is in your *swing*."

"What's wrong with it?"

Soup sighed. "I don't guess you know about rhythm count. You're not *counting* as you work. Champions usual do."

Leaning on my shovel, I stared at Soup. Perhaps, I was thinking, his Uncle Barney really *was* the state champion of all snow shovelers.

"Try it again," Soup said. "Only this time, divide your stroke into four beats."

"How?"

"One, shove your shovel under the snow as far as it'll go, so's you'll heft up a full load. Two, pick it up by using your legs and bending your knees a bit. Three, chuck the snow to one side, using swing. Four, bring back the empty shovel."

The way Soup explained, it certain sounded simple enough to master. Maybe, if I got real good at it, *I'd* be the state champ someday, just like Soup's Uncle Barney.

"Don't think about the *work*," said Soup. "You have to concentrate on the *counting*. So, to make it quicker for you to get the hang of it, we'll merely divide the problem. You handle the shovel, and *I'll count*. Ready?"

"Ready," I said.

"Now don't start," Soup said, "until I give you the signal, at the count of *one*. Get yourself set, be sure to brace your feet proper, and concentrate on rhythm."

"Okay," I told Soup as I braced my feet, my mittens taking a fresh purchase on the shovel's handle.

"One!" said Soup.

My shovel plunged forward.

"Two!"

I lifted an extra-heavy load.

"Three!"

The shovel swung left, depositing the snow into higher territory.

"Four!"

Twisting my body back to a normal position, I was about to turn around to check with Soup, to ask whether or not I'd mastered the rhythm. But before I could rest my shovel, I heard Soup counting again. So I shoveled some more.

"One . . . two . . . three . . . four. That's almost perfect. One, two, three, four. Great! Now just a speck faster and with a bigger load. One, two, three, four. One-two-three-four. Onetwothreefour. One. Four. One-four, one-four, onefour."

Even though my back was near to breaking, I couldn't seem to force myself to quit. All I could hear was Soup's counting as I pretended I was winning a trophy as a champion snow shoveler.

My shovel seemed to be half beast, half machine as the snow almost flew from Miss Witherspoon's sidewalk. Somewhere, in my imagination, a crowd was cheering me on to victory, and Norma Jean Bissell was blowing me kisses.

"One, two, three, four."

Thunk!

The forward edge of my shovel bumped into something that felt quite hard. I looked up and saw that it was the post of Miss Witherspoon's mailbox. Turning around, and almost fainting from fatigue, I saw that Soup was smiling.

"Rob, I'd give almost anything in the whole world if my Uncle Barney could see you shovel snow. I bet he'd declare you the next champion, right here and now."

As my breath slowly returned, I helped myself to a fresh slab of thinking. Soup hadn't performed too much edging. In fact, none at all.

"But I did all the *work*, Soup."

"Never mind that," said Soup. "Because I'm your personal *coach* from now on. No, I don't guess I'll win any of the glory. *You'll* be the one who has to take the big silver trophy home. Not me. But you've got to make me a promise, Rob."

"Yeah? What's that?"

"When you final win your silver trophy as the new State Champion, you'll at least mention the fact that I'm your coach—and give me a tiny little share of your victory."

I smiled. "Sure," I said.

As I collapsed onto a bank of snow, Soup stood there with a grin on his face. It was sort of strange, I was thinking, because *Soup* wasn't going to be the State Champion or win a trophy. *I* was.

Something caught my eye.

It turned out to be Miss Witherspoon, in her winter coat and galoshes, coming out of her front door and carrying her pocketbook. She paused, inspecting our hurried and edgeless job, then came to where Soup and I were, at her roadside mailbox.

As she opened her pocketbook, Soup extended his hand, in an eager gesture for our reward. But that was when Soup Vinson was rewarded with nothing but a cold glare from Miss Witherspoon.

"Here you are, Robert," she said, handing me a whole *quarter!* "Good job. I watched you do it *all* from my window. And *you* deserve all the money."

As he heard her, my pal's mouth fell open. "Miss Witherspoon," Soup asked her, "don't *I* get anything?"

Miss Witherspoon nodded. "Oh, indeed you do, Luther."

Soup started to grin, until she pointed to the snow-covered sidewalks next door. Looking at Soup, she smiled.

"What do I get?" Soup asked her.

"On someone else's sidewalk," she said sweetly, "you get another chance."

4

"That's it," said Soup. "Our last sidewalk."

It was only the middle of the afternoon, yet my back was starting to feel as though we'd been shoveling snow since early July.

Leaning against my shovel, I let out a big sigh. We'd cleared eleven sidewalks. I felt even more tired when I noticed that Soup appeared to be fresher than morning. Edging, I concluded, was lighter than shoveling.

"Let's go home, Soup. It'll be time for chores, and I can't afford to miss *those*. Not this close to Christmas and a possible BB gun."

We divided our change into equal shares: half for my shoveling; half for Soup's edging, coaching, and counting. But I kept Miss Witherspoon's quarter.

He grinned. "Rob, old top, I know the very thing to brighten our sagging winter spirits," Soup said as he pocketed his take.

"What's that?"

"A slide down the Double Zoomer," said Soup. "Come on. I'll race ya to the bottom."

Parking our shovels in a mound of snow at the village square, Soup and I took ourselves a long running start, hit the ice, and down the hill we slid, standing up and side by side on the twin tracks of polished ice. We slid all the way down and then coasted to a stop on the ice of the lake.

"Wow," I said. "The ice on the Double Zoomer seems to freeze faster every year."

As we stood on the frozen surface of Lake Champlain, Soup looked north. "That's because of the north wind, Pa says. He claims the wind is stiffer this December."

I couldn't argue. Looking north toward Canada, I had to blink my eyes as the wind was really whipping our way.

"I'm cold, Soup. Let's get going home."

We collected our two shovels and started to leave town the back way, along the railroad track. The houses nearby looked more than shabby. Most of them were shacks of unpainted wood, with no curtains in the windows. And some of the windows were covered over with rectangles of black tarpaper. None of the crusty doors sported even as much as a Christmas wreath.

Soup pointed at one of the shacks. "I know who lives there."

"So do I," I said. "The Tidwells."

"But just Ally and his ma," Soup said. "I happened to overhear Pa tell Ma that Ally's father, Jack Tidwell, left and ran away. His ma's sickly. But she takes in washing when she's able."

As Soup spoke, I stared at the Tidwell place. Their shack looked in worse shape than all the others. Seeing it made me realize why Ally Tidwell didn't believe much in Santa Claus or Christmas. Looking at his beat-up house, I wondered how Ally could believe in anything at all, except poverty.

Soup was quiet, for once, and I had a hunch that he was thinking about Ally too, and how poor the Tidwells really were.

We headed for home.

Below us lay the railroad tracks, in a deep gully, with ledges like steps on either side. We were now two ledges above the train tracks. Looking down, I spotted two people, a grown-up and a kid, carrying a sack. Bending over, they picked up lumps of coal that had tumbled from the tender, the coal bin that rode behind the locomotive. Along the tracks, black hunks of coal freckled the gray, dirty snow.

"Hey," said Soup, "it's Ally and his ma." His voice softened. "I don't guess the Tidwells can afford to buy any fuel to burn, to keep warm."

Before I could answer, I saw two more people. They stood on a ledge below us, off to our left, but above where Ally and Mrs. Tidwell hunted for coal. They were kids who had also spotted the Tidwells. It was Eddy Tacker and Janice Riker. Neither one had seen Soup or me. They were throwing hard hunks of snow down at Ally and his mother. One of the chunks of snow hit Mrs. Tidwell, and Ally put his arm around her.

As the Tidwells ran toward their shack, Soup picked up snow to help Ally and his ma. I did too. Maybe we could help them get away safely. We could easily outrun the two others.

Neither Soup nor I got to throw even one hunk of snow at Janice or Eddy because a big voice suddenly boomed.

"Hey, you @#*$% kids!"

Soup and I looked around to see an enormous man, who was cussing and chasing Janice and Eddy away. He stood on the ledge above them, near where we stood. Seeing both Eddy and Janice turn tail and run made me smile.

I recognized the man who'd run them off. Everyone in town knew him. His name was Stanley Dubinsky, but folks all called him Slosh. He was the owner of Slosh's Hot-Time Pool Parlor. People said that Slosh weighed almost three hundred pounds and stood near to six and a half feet tall. To me, he looked even bigger.

Mr. Dubinsky was still cussing at Janice and Eddy. "Beat it! Ain't you doggone kids got no sense of what's decent? Get the @#*$% out of here!"

Eddy and Janice fled for their lives.

But then the worst happened. Turning, Mr. Dubinsky spotted Soup and me, holding the hunks of snow that we intended to use against Eddy and Janice, to be on the Tidwells' side. Mr. Dubinsky's face turned even redder.

"Hey! How come all of you @#*$% kids gotta act so @#*$% mean?"

He headed our way, snarling.

"Run," said Soup.

I tried. But my feet wouldn't budge even an inch. Soup couldn't run either. Meanwhile, Mr. Slosh Dubinsky was smoking our way, looking taller and fatter and meaner with every step. As he came closer it was impossible to believe that Slosh was only one individual. Actually, he didn't look like a person. He looked more the size of a refrigerator.

As he stopped and stared down at Soup and me, everything that I had ever heard about Mr. Slosh Dubinsky came suddenly to mind. Folks claimed he had stopped wrestling because he'd broken the bones and mashed the noses of too many other guys. Rumor had it that his parents had been a grizzly bear and a bulldozer.

He now stood directly before us, still cussing, his kneecap almost as high as my chin.

His white beard shook with outrage. A giant paw reached out to seize the front of my coat, and suddenly my feet no longer rested in snow. Soup was being held thusly in the air by my side.

"Shame on youse two boys," Mr. Dubinsky growled. "Throwing snow down at poor people who's pickin' up coal."

As his talons released us, Soup and I fell, landing in the crusty snow. High above me, all I could see was a pair of bright blue eyes, a great white beard, and a nose that only a violent temper could have reddened to the hue of a taillight.

"We didn't do it," Soup said weakly.

"No," I croaked. "We were going to help the Tidwells. Honest. We're in school with Ally."

"He's our friend," said Soup.

Mr. Dubinsky hauled in a lung-filling breath and then let it out in a blast that seemed more like a steamy gale. "Are you @#*$% kids telling me the @#*$% truth?" he roared at us.

Soup and I both nodded, again informing Mr. Dubinsky that we were intending to help Ally and his mother to escape from Janice and Eddy.

"Ally doesn't have any friends," Soup said, "except for Rob and me. We aren't ashamed to be his pals."

"We're proud of it," I said.

Right then, I saw a sight I'd never seen before. And it would be an experience I'd remember, even if I lived to turn older than Miss Witherspoon.

Slosh Dubinsky smiled.

5

"I wrote mine," Soup whispered.

Like usual, the two of us were sitting in school, side by side on a bench, and behind one desk. It was Monday.

"Rob, did you hand in yours?"

"Yup," I told him. "What there was of it."

Up front, Miss Kelly was seated behind her desk, grading our themes. But then she looked up and tapped her shoe on the floor, three times, to warn Soup and me that we were supposed to be studying our geography, without conversation.

A geography book, I had long ago decided, was a dull thing to look at, especially when I could steal a secret glance at Norma Jean Bissell. Hardly an easy feat, as she sat several rows away and slightly to the rear.

To be honest about it, I sneaked a look at Norma Jean Bissell no fewer than three hundred times during any given school day. Soup usually noticed my doing it and would feign an acute spasm of gastric disorder.

As I looked again at Norma Jean, a familiar feeling seemed to gnaw at my interior glands and organs. It was a suffering somewhat akin to what I felt whenever I saw an Official Buck Jones Daisy Repeater BB Gun in the hardware store window. Yet on this particular afternoon, my longings for Norma Jean or Buck Jones offered little solace. I was too worried about my composition, which I had turned in early this morning.

Soup flipped over a geographical page. No matter. I wasn't reading, or even caring, about the difference between Bolivia and boll weevils.

At her desk, Miss Kelly still busied herself with evaluating our themes. But then she stood, holding up a familiar-looking composition. "There seems to be," Miss Kelly announced, "no name on this particularly untidy paper. And it is less than *one* page. Whose is it?"

I spoke up. "It might be mine, Miss Kelly." I faked a smile. "Uh, maybe I sort of forgot to sign my name."

Eyeing my paper once again, Miss Kelly placed my literary offering on top of the pile. "Robert Peck, you will please remain after school."

"Yes'm," I squeaked.

"You're in for it now," said Soup. "You didn't even write one full page. I wrote two."

Don't panic, I told myself. There might be a clever escape hatch from punishment. Reaching into a pocket, I extracted a large white hanky, then tied it around my right hand, so it looked like a bandage.

"You'll still get the ruler," Soup whispered. "She'll never fall for *that* puny excuse."

"How do *you* know?"

Soup grinned. "I already tried it, last April, when you were home with the measles."

The afternoon dragged. But I knew the school day was limping to its frazzled finish when I saw Miss Kelly take her usual two Anacin tablets. It was hard to figure why Miss Kelly always looked so worn out and beat up by day's end. She was *only* the teacher. We *kids* did all the work.

Promptly at three o'clock, my fellow pupils lined up to shake our teacher's hand and wish her a good night. As the last winter-protected, woolen-bundled scholar took his leave, Miss Kelly closed the heavy storm door, walked slowly to her desk, and then sat.

This, I knew, was my cue.

Rising from my bench, I marched forward with leaden steps, again forcing my confident smile. Miss Kelly, however, was not smiling at all. With a stern expression she coldly assessed the hanky now furled about my hand.

"What's the matter?" Miss Kelly asked me, in a tone that had doubted many a freckled faker.

Raising my right hand, I winced, pretending to fight the pain. "This? Oh, I possible sprained it working so hard, shoveling snow on Saturday." It was an outright lie. "I can hardly move it at all, it hurts so doggone much." Another boldface falsehood.

"That is your *writing hand*," said Miss Kelly, "I presume."

"Yes'm. So, on Sunday, after I *broke* my hand—"

Miss Kelly raised one eyebrow with a well-practiced gesture. I'd seen her do it many times. It was her silent way of informing you that she disbelieved the story she was hearing.

"You *broke* it?"

"Well, maybe I actual didn't break the bone

clear through. It's possible I just sort of *sprained* it some."

"And," my teacher said, "when Sunday evening came, last night, your tormented hand prevented you from writing two pages. So you wrote less than half a page."

"Yes'm."

The ruler lay in front of her, on the desk and in plain sight. Reaching my left hand upward, I scratched the back of my neck, where all three of my sweaters were starting to itch me. Then, sucking in a deep breath, I told Miss Kelly the biggest and rottenest lie of my entire life.

"Uh, I had to do most of it with my left hand. Because it hurt so furious to write normal that I just about screamed on every letter. That's how come my theme looks so sloppy."

"I see." Miss Kelly looked down at the one puny paragraph that I'd submitted, instead of two full pages. "Perhaps that is the reason, Robert, that your untidy penmanship is so illegible, and that your composition is decorated so profusely with inkblots."

As I nodded, my throat began to rehash the unchewed tuna fish sandwich that I'd bolted for lunch, as well as the apple and a hunk of baking chocolate that I'd swiped from Mama's pantry.

Miss Kelly handed me my theme. "Robert, as I found your scrawling and scratching impossible to read, perhaps you will be so kind as to read it to me. Aloud please."

With trembling hands, as well as a loosening bandage, I took my theme from Miss Kelly and read it to her.

What I Wish for Christmas

I wish the Tidwells didn't have to be so poor and live in a dirty old shack without a wreath on the door. They have to pick up railroad coal to burn. I wish Ally Tidwell had a warm bed, like mine, and lots to eat because he's so skinny. Most of all, I want to do something so Ally will believe there's a Christmas.

It wasn't two pages.

I'd only written a few dumb old words, but I wanted to tell Miss Kelly that my words weren't a lie, because it was sort of what I wished for Christmas. And when I'd written my paragraph, I wasn't thinking even once about getting a BB gun.

But I lied to her about my hand. Rob, I told myself silently, you're a real lousy kid.

My stomach was now waltzing with a tuna fish. Around and around it danced, circling faster and faster, whirling and climbing, a storm of seething chocolate, apple, tuna fish, fibs, and fakery.

It wasn't just today's lunch. As I remembered all the terrible lies I'd told Miss Kelly, my stomach seemed to be remembering every morsel I'd eaten since my weaning. It all lay there, seething within me. Years of Milky Ways, the cotton candy from last July's circus, gallons of root beer and cream soda, frankfurters from picnics, mustard now more molten than lava, relish, plus a penny or two I'd swallowed as a toddler. In my throat, I tasted bubble gum, jawbreakers (both red and black), birthday cake, charcoal beads of unpopped corn, and a cord of licorice logs.

As my teacher stared at me, all of it wanted to come up. Every bite, along with my heart, a lung or two, about seven feet of intestine, and both kidneys.

"Are you all right?" Miss Kelly asked.

"Yes'm," I moaned, knowing that any second I might cease to be a kid and become an erupting volcano.

Suddenly I knew why I was feeling so sick. It wasn't my lunch's fault. It was mine, because I'd told lies to Miss Kelly. So, I reasoned, maybe if lying made me feel so rotten, telling the truth would heal me well again.

"I told you a lie, Miss Kelly."

"Oh?" Again her eyebrow raised. "And now, Robert, you'd like to tell me the truth?"

I nodded, unable to speak.

Miss Kelly leaned back in her chair. "Perhaps," she said, "I can help. You really didn't damage your hand, even though you did shovel snow on Saturday. Today, you became upset when you realized what a mess you handed in."

She looked at my theme.

"Yes'm," I croaked. "What bothers me the most is—I lied to you so I wouldn't get the ruler. Maybe I ought to get it. Because what I handed in was the worst one."

Miss Kelly stood up. "Well, it was easily the messiest, and by far the shortest." She paused. "But you're mistaken about its being the worst." Miss Kelly walked around the desk to stand near me, looking down at me. "In one sense, your composition is the best."

I looked up at her. "The *best* one?"

Her hand touched my shoulder. "You lied to me; you were also lazy and quite untidy. All the other students, however, wrote about what they wanted for themselves. You wanted a Christmas for Ally. On the outside, your paper is a mess. But inside— it is about as bright and shiny as any Christmas wish could ever be. In a way, you have given me about the nicest gift that a teacher could ever receive."

"Honest?"

She nodded, then knelt to look me in the eyes. "Today, you taught me a lesson. Sometimes we teachers judge too quickly, seeing the surface, yet never valuing the hidden heart. Thank you, Robert."

As my crumpled theme was still in my hand, I looked at it. "Next time," I told her, "I'll try to do it neater, and longer. I'm real sorry it's so little."

Miss Kelly smiled at me, and spoke softly.

"Diamonds often are."

6

"Wheeeeeee!"

Soup and I were both yelling as we slid, after a running start, down the twin strips of ice known as the Double Zoomer. Every day, the ice seemed to be becoming slicker, faster, and more fun.

An elderly gentleman stood watching us. As we climbed back up the hill for another slide, he shook a warning finger.

"Boys, you best take caution on that ice. Maybe

you didn't yet hear what happened to Joe Sutter."

We stood still.

"What happened?" Soup asked him.

"Well, I just heard about it myself. Seems like Joe slipped on the ice and hurt himself. They say his leg'll be in a cast for nigh close to ten weeks."

"Is he in the hospital?" I asked.

"Sure is," the man answered. "A doggone shame, considering the Christmas Eve shindig." He shook his head. "It could near to ruin everything." He turned and walked away.

Soup looked at me. "Rob, old top. You and I better leg it over to Miss Boland's, and right sudden."

"How come?" I asked Soup as we ran.

"Because," he panted, "last year I suspected that the man who dressed up as Santa Claus was that big Joe Sutter guy."

We spotted Miss Boland near her house, parking her tiny Hoover car. We yelled to her. Hearing us, our county nurse turned and threw us a half-hearted wave, a gesture that lacked her customary exuberance.

Soup nudged me. "She knows."

As we approached, Miss Boland's face seemed to darken. Her entire body slumped into a position of defeat.

"We just heard about Mr. Sutter," said Soup.

"His leg's hurt and in a cast," I said.

Miss Boland glumly nodded.

"Maybe," said Soup, "Rob and I can help."

"How?" she asked.

"Well," said Soup, "I'd sort of guess you might be needing somebody else to take Mr. Sutter's place—and be *you know who*."

Miss Boland's eyebrows raised in surprise. "How in the name did you two rascals find out about all this?" She threw up her mittened hands. "Never mind. We certain can't discuss it out here in this freezing weather. Come on inside. We'll have ourselves some practical palaver."

Taking turns with the broom on Miss Boland's porch, the three of us attacked the snow off our boots, whisked ourselves tidy, then entered her little house. Miss Boland excused herself and waddled to her kitchen, returning in a minute or so, toting three steaming mugs.

"Hot cider," she told us. "It's warded off many a Vermont chill. So drink hearty."

The hot cider tasted super. Miss Boland had added a dash of spice that my tongue estimated was either cinnamon or nutmeg. Thanking her, Soup and I both admitted how yummy it tasted.

"Okay," said Soup, helping himself to a few more sips of hot cider, "we've got a problem, Miss Boland."

Her face fell. "Don't I know it. I just came from the hospital. Joe's in bed, straight out, with his leg pointed at the ceiling. Slipped on the ice, he says. You know where he lives, away out on Mulligan's Road."

I nodded. "Everybody says that Mulligan's Road is one of the most icy places in town because it's so near the lake."

"So," Miss Boland gestured with her hands, "there's no way we can postpone Christmas until February."

Soup grinned. "All we have to do," he said, "is scare up somebody else to play Santa."

Miss Boland paced the floor of her small parlor. "I can't think of anybody. Bert Motley's got the flu. Sam Crosetti is going out of town, and Olly Lester has turned me down three times today. Joe, Bert, Sam, and Olly are the only big, chubby guys that I can corner. The rest of the gents won't do because they're all leaner than string beans."

"Gosh," said Soup. "Now I'm starting to understand why you're so down in the dumps."

"Me too," I told her.

"Joe Sutter's such a jolly, good-natured fellow." Miss Boland halfway smiled. "Even though he can't be Santa Claus this year, Joe said we could borrow his Santa suit, which he keeps in his barn. I don't guess we'll need his sleigh, now that Joe won't be available to drive it." Her face saddened. "Trouble is, we don't have a guy to . . ."

Miss Boland snapped her fingers.

"I got it! I'll telephone my second cousin who

lives north of here, up in Thurgood. His name's Harley Thatcher, and I know *he'll* make a cracking good Santa. He hasn't missed a meal in thirty years."

Leaping to the phone, Miss Boland began to click the hook with an impatient finger. "Myrtle, it's me. I'd like to call long distance." Miss Boland paused. "Yes, I know it'll cost extra, but I'll spring. Connect me with number thirty-four in Thurgood."

Soup and I waited.

"Helen, is that you? Please put Harley on the wire, will ya?" Pause. "He's out to the barn? Then run fetch him, and quick." Longer pause. "Darn it, this'll gouge me a fortune. Harley, that you?" Pause. "How would you like to ramble down here to Learning on Christmas Eve and dress up as Santa Claus?" Short pause. "You wouldn't." Pause. "You're singing in the church choir. Okay, so long, and love to Helen."

"Scratch one more off the list," said Soup.

"There's got to be *somebody*," I said.

"But *who?*" asked Miss Boland.

"Well," I said, "what about Mr. Jubert?"

Miss Boland winced. "Not hardly. Santa Claus is supposed to be jolly, and Mr. Jubert hasn't smiled since Emma left him. But then she came back."

Soup said, "You could always ask Vernal Wilcox."

"Not a chance," Miss Boland told us. "The trouble with Vernal is that he'll insist on playing 'Silent Night' on the saxophone. He'll be really sore if we don't ask him to play. And if he blows that sorry contraption, everyone else'll be sore. Unless we pass out earmuffs."

"But," said Soup, "we've got to get *somebody* to be Santa."

"What about Arnold Kesky?" I asked.

Miss Boland looked surprised. "He's thinner than a rail on a hot-weather diet."

"Yup," I said, "but Arnold doesn't play the saxophone. I think he plays the cornet."

"Phil Tabor plays the trombone," said Soup.

Miss Boland near to screamed. "Boys, boys— we're not putting a *band* together. All we're doing is trying to finger somebody to play Santa, not a musical instrument."

"Maybe," said Soup, "I could sort of convince my pa into playing Santa Claus."

Miss Boland snorted. "Your pa happens to be leaner than Arnold Kesky, in case you haven't noticed of recent."

Soup jumped to his feet and paced the floor while Miss Boland sat a spell and gulped her hot cider which was, by this time, cold.

"I've just thought of somebody," I said.

"Who?" Miss Boland asked me.

"Harold Spencer. He's big and chubby, and he

doesn't play the cornet or the saxophone."

Miss Boland frowned. "No dice. Harold's in charge of stringing the lights on the big spruce tree. He's got enough to tackle already."

"Okay," I said, "we don't ask Harold Spencer."

Soup still paced the floor. "We're not thinking hard enough," he said. "For sure and certain, there's just got to be *somebody* in the town of Learning who could be a Santa Claus."

"But who?" asked Miss Boland. "I already drove out to chase down Stilson Wheeler, but he's moved clear out of town. Besides, he might've made a poor Santa, now that I really consider it."

"Why?" asked Soup.

"He chews tobacco. Little kids," said Miss Boland, "won't believe in a Santa Claus who's got tobacco juice running down into his whiskers. Besides, right in the middle of his ho-ho-ho, he'd probable have to spit."

Right then, I was witness to something quite unusual. Soup suddenly leaped high into the air, executed an incredible back flip, and landed cleanly.

"I got it!" he yelped.

"Who?" Miss Boland and I asked.

"I've got the perfect person to play the part of Santa Claus on Christmas Eve."

"Well," said Miss Boland, "tell us."

Soup grinned. "Mr. Slosh Dubinsky."

Miss Boland screamed, choking on her cider,

and her face turned whiter than a midnight ghost. "No," she whispered, when she could finally speak. "Slosh Dubinsky is probable the meanest guy in town. Not to mention his cussing. And he positively *hates kids*."

As she said it, I didn't quite agree with Miss Boland, because I was remembering how Slosh was trying to protect the Tidwells. My mother usual insisted that there was *good* inside everybody. Mama couldn't be wrong. And, I was thinking, Mr. Slosh Dubinsky couldn't be all bad, the way some folks claimed.

"But," said Soup, "he's perfect for the part."

"Why?" asked Miss Boland.

Soup bent a wider grin. "Mr. Slosh Dubinsky is perfect because it so happens that *he's the only one we've got.*"

Miss Boland groaned. "Luther," she said at last to Soup, "you're probable correct. Slosh Dubinsky would make an impossible Santa, but right now, he's our last chance."

Soup nodded.

"However," said Miss Boland, "you won't saddle *me* with going into that filthy pool parlor of his. I refuse to be the goat who has to ask a favor of that dreadful man. Ladies can't go into places like that."

"Who'll do it?" I asked.

"Well," said Miss Boland, "the fewer people who

know about this caper, the better." Her eyes narrowed, staring at Soup and me. Then came the real shocker. She told us who would have to go face big Slosh and convince him to be our Santa Claus. *"You two,"* she said firmly.

Soup and I both spilled our cider.

"This is it," said Soup.

It was the next day, after school, and the two of us stood nervously on Main Street, looking up at a sign. The blood-red letters read:

SLOSH'S HOT-TIME POOL PARLOR

The butterflies in my stomach now seemed to be firing machine guns. I'd heard that this was the roughest and toughest hangout in town. Rumor persisted that, in Slosh's, a guy who still had both ears and all his teeth was called a sissy.

Even though I was wearing mittens, I started to gnaw on my fingernails.

"Rob," said Soup, "maybe we ought to draw

straws, to see which one of us goes inside to ask him. And I hope it won't be Soup Vinson who loses."

"Maybe," I said, praying that it wouldn't be Rob Peck who had to open that big black door to face Mr. Stanley Dubinsky, "we could *both* go in."

Slosh's Hot-Time Pool Parlor was the one local establishment into which, my mother had warned me, I was *never* to set foot. Soup's mother had told him the same, threatening that if *he* ventured inside, his behind would enjoy a hot-time of its own.

Aunt Carrie, I clearly recalled as I now stared at Slosh's door, had also delivered a lengthy and vehement sermon on the evils of Slosh's Hot-Time Pool Parlor, and about pocket billiards in general. "Pool balls," Aunt Carrie concluded, "are the Devil's rosary."

"Are you scared?" I asked Soup.

"No, I'm not scared."

"Me too," I admitted.

Yet, with a cautious tread, up the three creaking stairs we climbed, and we now faced the big black door that warned: MEN ONLY.

"You knock," Soup told me.

"Not me. Slosh was *your* idea."

After a short debate on who would handle the knocking, we both knuckled softly. But all we heard in response was a roar of deep men-only laughter, from inside.

"Maybe they didn't hear us," said Soup.

We knocked again. But nobody came to welcome us into Slosh's forbidden fortress of fun.

"Let's go inside," Soup said. "You go first."

I took a deep breath. "Okay, but you'd darn well better come along too."

As Soup turned the knob, I pushed. Nothing happened, so we both pushed and the door yielded. A pungent men-only aroma of tobacco smoke and beverages, which I couldn't identify as soda pop, tortured my nostrils.

"It's sort of *dark* in there," I told Soup as the crack of the door widened and a sharp clack of scattering pool balls punctured my ears.

Somebody swore.

Yet the cuss words hadn't come from a male voice. It was definitely a lady who had employed the vibrant vocabulary. Mustering my spunk, I risked a stealthy advance of one more inch.

"Are you going in?" Soup asked me.

"Not unless you push me."

He pushed, and into the murky atmosphere we crept. I sure was grateful that Soup had come too; even though he, like I, had been probable enticed more by curiosity than courage.

Pool balls clattered, and once again I heard a fascinating blend of lewdity and laughter.

"Ya missed, Rosie," a male voice chided.

A large lady in a red satiny dress, whom I presumed to be Rosie herself, suddenly turned around and spotted us as Soup and I approached a big brown pool table. Her cheeks, lips, and hair were three different colors. Yet all entirely red. A thin cigar smoldered from a corner of Rosie's painted mouth.

I swallowed, hearing Soup do the same. Unable to hold my breath any longer, I breathed, feeling as though I was playing a dirty trick on my lungs.

"Slosh!" snarled Rosie through clenched teeth as she leaned on her cue stick and flicked her cigar. "Ya got company."

One of the big lumberjacks spat at a spittoon, missed, then pointed at us and laughed. "Maybe them two young sports come to see *you*, Rosie." But the man was promptly silenced by a swift and well-aimed jab of Rosie's cue stick. As the wounded victim spilled his sudsy beverage, the other men howled with appreciation.

"HEY!"

All heads turned to see Mr. Slosh Dubinsky. I blinked. Every guy in the place was big, yet Mr. Dubinsky towered mightier than any two of them. And wider.

"What in the @#*$% are you @#*$% kids doing in this @#*$% place?" he inquired.

"Go ahead and ask him," Soup whispered.

Mr. Dubinsky glared at Soup. "What's your name, kid?"

"Robert Peck," said Luther Vinson.

Slosh then looked down at me.

"Luther Vinson" was all I could think of to say, so I said it.

"Well," growled Mr. Dubinsky, "you @#*$% small fry ain't allowed in this @#*$% place. So get the @#$% out."

"We came," I gurgled, "for a favor."

One of the millworkers at another pool table let out a loud laugh. "Rosie," he yelled, "your gentlemen friends is either over seventy or under ten. *Haw, haw, haw.*"

Lifting a pool ball from its bed of green felt, Rosie wound up and then released one beauty of a sidearm curve, a pitch that would have earned her a uniform on any team in the major leagues. As the ball thudded into the heckler's stomach, his eyes crossed.

"What kind of a @#*$% favor?" asked Slosh Dubinsky in a whisper that could have been heard clearly in a sawmill.

Soup nudged him. "Tell him."

Taking a deep breath, I told him. I explained our mission in detail. "Mr. Dubinsky," I said, "it seems like Joe Sutter slipped on the ice. Miss Boland's cousin up in Thurgood sings in the choir, Bert Motley's got the flu, Mr. Jubert doesn't smile because Emma came back, and we've already heard Vernal Wilcox's saxophone. Mr. Kesky is too skinny, and Stilson Wheeler moved out of town."

The frown on Mr. Dubinsky's face gradually untwisted into an expression of confusion. He scratched his beard with a giant paw.

"I don't get it, kid. What in the name of @#*$% has all that @#*$% stuff got to do with me?"

"Well," I gulped, "we really need somebody to be Santa on Christmas Eve, because everybody we asked has said *no*. You're our last chance. Please be our Santa Claus."

As I said it, the entire congregation of mill-workers, lumberjacks, and Rosie all exploded into howls. Giant index fingers, the size of salamis, pointed at Slosh. Huge fangs parted to hoot at him in a rowdy round of ridicule. The happy hollering persisted until Mr. Dubinsky entered his decorous plea for quietude.

"All you @#*$% people shut the @#*$% up."

They stilled, except for one large lumberman who persisted in twitting the proprietor. But then he too became silent when Slosh gently covered the man's entire head and neck with an inverted and rapidly emptying spittoon.

"We're next," I heard Soup say.

Glaring down at us, Mr. Stanley Dubinsky, now posing as the typical concerned citizen, startled me with his modest request for further information.

"Why in the @#$% do you @#$% kids think I'd wanna dress up in some @#$% red suit and pretend I'm a @#$% Santa Claus?"

I swallowed.

"Because," I told him in a weak whisper, "some of the kids in town don't get much of a Christmas. To a kid like Ally Tidwell, who has to pick up coal along the railroad tracks, if you could be Santa it would mean a lot, Mr. Dubinsky—to Ally and to his mother."

Some of the pool shooters laughed, until Slosh wordlessly begged for silence by throwing a chair. He scratched his fluffy white beard again. "Yeah," he said softly. "Being poor like them Tidwells ain't no @#$% fun. I was a poor kid, and as I recall, it was a doggone sorry deal."

"It would be the greatest thing you ever did, Mr. Dubinsky," I said. "Honest, it would."

That became the moment when I received the most jarring shock of my entire life. Mr. Slosh Dubinsky bent down and squinted at me with one bloodshot eye, exhaling a stained breath, the fumes of which could have peeled away varnish.

"I'll do it, Luther," he whispered.

8

"Rob?"

My coat was on, and my mittened hand was reaching for the kitchen door, ready to escape, just as I heard my mother calling my name.

"I'm here, Mama."

"Where are you going at this hour?"

"Oh, just uproad to Soup's," I told my mother, bending the truth.

"Remember," she cautioned, "it's dark outside, and cold, and it'll be your bedtime soon. Be a good lad because Christmas is coming."

My hopeful mind envisioned Mama and Papa lovingly wrapping an Official Buck Jones Daisy Repeater BB Gun, fresh from the window of Harry's Hardware Store, a gift for their adorable son.

"There's school tomorrow," she added.

"Right. So I'll be back in good season."

Outside, I bolted uproad in the direction of Soup's, but never got there. Soup, also on a dead run, met me halfway. Out of breath, he told me that he'd informed his folks that he was coming to the Pecks'.

"So far so good," I said. "But what's your secret plan? How come you suggested that we sneak out tonight?"

"Rob, old top, just follow me."

I asked few further questions. Whatever it was that Luther Wesley Vinson was scheming, his furtivity he would unfold in his own casual way. As I trudged along the snow-packed road at his side, Soup abruptly turned north at a corner where another road met ours.

"Where are we going, Soup?"

"Well, sort of up Mulligan's Road."

I stopped. "Why?"

"We have to borrow Mr. Sutter's red Santa suit in order to help Miss Boland. And maybe we might even improve her overall plan for Christmas Eve. I'm cooking up a secret plan of my own. You heard Miss Boland tell us that we had permission to use Mr. Sutter's red suit."

I nodded. Soup was right about that. Yet the part that made me itch was the fact that *we* were borrowing it. As we walked, I mentioned that to Soup.

"Weren't you listening?" he asked. "Miss Boland's got so much else to do, she's sort of turned the Santa Claus preparation over to us, including getting Slosh Dubinsky ready."

"Okay," I said.

Along most of Mulligan's Road, the farmhouses were already dark. No lights burned within, and no windows invitingly yellowed. Vermonters retire right after prayers, which follow supper, which follows chores, which follow a long day of labor, which, on a list of farming priorities, is put *before* anything else.

The last house on the lakeside road sat behind a mailbox that modestly stated, in faint letters, the name of its one large resident:

SUTTER, it said.

I stopped again. "I don't like it. Especially the part where you said you had some kind of a secret plan of your own." Something inside was warning me that Soup was up to doing more than merely borrowing a Santa suit.

"You will, Rob. It's one of my wildest ideas."

Still standing by the mailbox, I said, "Your wild ideas usual land us smack into a mess of trouble. I don't guess I want to play a part in any dumb *prank*. Not this close to Christmas." If anything could defeat my getting a BB gun, I was thinking, it would be one of Soup's insane schemes.

Soup turned. "It's not a prank. We're doing a *favor* for Miss Boland. We're borrowing a Santa suit. Actually we're doing most of the favor for Slosh Dubinsky."

As Soup spoke the name, I shuddered, and not from the north wind that was blowing down nearby Lake Champlain. However, why I followed Luther Vinson behind the house and to Mr. Sutter's barn I will never know. *Favors* performed by Soup were usual done for himself, not for Miss Boland, Mr. Dubinsky, or me.

There's something eerie about the way a heavy barn door squeaks at night. The moon had scooted behind a cloud, and the darkness seemed to accentuate the spooky creaking of the door. It groaned like a wailing spirit.

"Good," said Soup. "In we go."

"It's dark in this place. And creepy."

"Not for long." Soup lit a match, which was immediately blown out by the whipping wind. "Rob, did you see it?"

"See what?"

"Over yonder. There's Mr. Sutter's red sleigh." He lit another match, which sputtered briefly and died. "Now all we need is to find several more useful items and we're all set. Ah, here's his Santa suit. Coat, pants, and hat." He struck a third match.

"Good," I said. "Mr. Sutter told Miss Boland that it was okay to use his Santa suit. So, let's collect it and head for home."

"Not just yet," said Soup. He wasn't looking at

the red suit. Instead, he was eyeing Mr. Sutter's sleigh.

"Hold on," I told Soup. "Miss Boland said we could borrow the Santa suit, but later she claimed we wouldn't need the sleigh. Even if we did, we don't have any horses. And we'd need *oxen* to pull Mr. Dubinsky."

Soup said nothing. He merely lit another match, studied the sleigh, then blew out the match and became quite busy. Finding a lantern, he lit it, then pulled a strange piece of paper from his pocket and unfolded it. It looked like some kind of an odd drawing with lines on it.

"What are you doing, Soup?"

"Thinking."

"I don't like it when you think. Because it always means we'll get ourselves in trouble."

"Rob, old top, this won't be any trouble at all. Not if my engineering proves to be accurate."

Without another word, Soup began to collect several articles that he found, one by one, in Mr. Sutter's barn. Some tangled wire, a gigantic horse blanket, several bean poles, coils of old rope, plus a jingling set of sleigh bells. He loaded each article into the sleigh.

"There," he said.

"Soup, what's all this junk for?"

He grinned. "Just for fun," he said. "And I know it'll work. It can't miss."

"You said it has something to do with our plans for Christmas Eve," I said.

His grin extended. "Practically everything. In fact, it'll turn an ordinary Santa into a super Santa in a sleigh. And you and I shall be riding beside him during our triumphant entry into Learning."

"I don't like it," I said. "Miss Boland said that all we'd have to borrow was the Santa suit."

Soup checked all of the so-called equipment that he'd busily assembled. "You'll see," he told me. "Just be patient. I wouldn't dream of hogging all the glory on Christmas Eve. Not without my good old buddy Rob Peck."

The way he said it made me grateful that I had Luther Wesley Vinson for a pal, despite his weird plans for impending doom. To be certain, Soup could be a devilish dilemma at times, yet never dull. Somehow he was always a red cherry atop my ice cream sundae.

Soup had now climbed into the sleigh, and on his head he was wearing Mr. Sutter's red Santa hat. "That's it," he told me. "I think we've collected just about every item we'll need for the final construction."

"What are we going to construct? Is it some nutty kind of a machine?"

Soup beamed. "One nifty surprise."

"I s'pose," I told Soup, "it's mainly going to be for Mr. Dubinsky, like you earlier said." Yet somehow I suspected otherwise.

"Well," said Soup, "I sort of thought it would be a whole lot of fun if we *all* made a sleigh-bell entrance for Santa on Christmas Eve—as a favor to Mr. Dubinsky."

Sighing, I looked at the sleigh and its strange load, but little of it made any sense. None, in fact. "Soup," I said, "I'm really not certain we ought to attempt whatever it is you're planning."

Staring down from the junk-piled sleigh seat, Soup shot me a disappointed look. "Rob, you want Norma Jean Bissell to admire you as we make a big impression on Christmas Eve, don't you?"

I did.

My heart danced at the very mention of Norma Jean's name. But as I assessed the little red sleigh, which now looked like a junk wagon, I doubted the seat would hold much more of a cargo than Santa Dubinsky, he of considerable measure. And, without horses, I wondered how Soup planned to bring the sleigh to town.

Soup seemed to be reading my thoughts.

"Don't worry," he told me, removing the Santa hat from his head and replacing it with his own purple wool.

Usually, I'm not much of a worrywart. Except when a lunatic such as Luther Vinson tells me not to worry, at which time I start worrying until my ears ring.

As I walked around the sleigh, looking at it in the amber lantern light, I told Soup that I still couldn't fathom how he was planning to use all the wire, a horse blanket, bean poles, old rope, and sleigh bells.

Soup chuckled. "Oh, you'll see," he said. "It's only a minor variation in Miss Boland's plan. We won't have to borrow the red Santa suit tonight."

"We won't?"

"No," said Soup. "Just trust me. You won't believe what we're really going to do. And you'll really impress Norma Jean."

He was baiting the hook again, using Norma Jean Bissell as the enticing worm. What's more, he continued to do so while we were blowing out the lantern and closing Mr. Sutter's barn. We left the Santa suit in the sleigh. As for the mysterious machine, Soup said nothing more on the way home. Whenever I'd probe for a direct explanation, Soup only responded by singing a verse from a song he was composing. The name of his song was "Disaster."

"Oh . . . a . . . daredevil cowboy named Milton Beware
Could juggle five dynamite sticks in the air.
But they found his sombrero
In Rio Janeiro,
And his fanny at old Rutland Fair."

Later, in bed, no matter how often I'd punch my pillow, I couldn't fall asleep. Finally, out of sheer exhaustion, I drifted off and into one horror of a nightmare. It was a Christmas party. Miss Boland, as Santa, rode a strange machine, constructed from bean poles, wire, and a horse blanket. Eddy Tacker, Janice Riker, and Soup seemed to be riding three camels, dressed as the Three Wise Men.

Worse yet, in three-part harmony, the camels were merrily singing Soup's crazy song.

"Disaster."

9

It came, our final day of school.

Miss Kelly stood before us. We also were standing, sharing our limited supply of scruffy songbooks, yet singing fit to bust.

To the rhythm of Miss Kelly's ruler and its swinging cadence, our twenty-eight cherubic voices were now ringing as one. Our stuffed-up noses and sore throats momentarily forgotten, we merrily warbled all the anthems we knew about Christmas.

> *"You'll be seeing Mister Claus.*
> *Here's the reason. It's because . . .*
> *Santa's on his way to town."*

As I looked at Soup, I realized that he, I, and Miss Boland were possible the only ones who knew that this season's Santa would be none other than the cussing proprietor of Slosh's Hot-Time Pool

Parlor. Miss Boland had sworn us to absolute secrecy, claiming that perhaps a few of Learning's parents might be offended that such an unworthy member of our saintly community would dare to keynote our Yuletide festivities.

Our singing continued, verse upon endless verse, with Janice Riker singing louder than everyone else combined.

She also possessed the most rasping voice, one that rarely kept pace with the rest of us. Janice sang a measure behind. Her voice didn't actually produce a tone. It sounded more like a tire puncture. Her better notes reminded me of a chain saw calling to its mate. Nonetheless, I had to give old Janice credit for her seasonal enthusiasm.

Mercifully for the sake of the composer, who might have been listening somewhere (Janice could have been heard in Idaho), our slaughtering of "Santa's On His Way to Town" chugged to its wheezing end at last. All voices but one blended in a final *"tooooooo toowwwwnnnn."*

We stopped.

"To town," sang Janice Riker.

Nobody laughed. Not at Janice, because staying alive for Christmas seemed, to all the rest of the class, rather important.

We also sang "God Is Love."

During this particular song, however, my devotions were not dwelling on God. Because whenever we sang the word *love,* I'd steal a furtive look at

Norma Jean Bissell. Once she even looked at me, and I felt both of my cheeks turning redder than Christmas.

Earlier in the season, I'd planned to buy a present to give Norma Jean, but the cold facts of local retailing altered my intentions. After carefully assessing the price tags on rattraps, laxatives, and mothballs, the three gifts for my family, I realized that I'd barely have enough of my shoveling money to squeak by.

Next year, I silently promised, I'd perform the snow shoveling and splurge a trip to Moe's Jewelry, with Norma Jean in mind.

Ally Tidwell was singing too. It made me feel right happy to watch him sing, and I wanted to do something nice for Ally, as well as for Norma Jean. Before school, Ally had told me that he'd also shoveled snow for people, and had earned enough to buy a cheese for his mother.

As I stared at Ally, I noticed that his hands appeared a mite dirty. Yet, as he sang "God Is Love," his face looked cleaner than a star.

In the corner of our school's one and only room leaned our three-foot-high Christmas tree, in a bucket of water. Branches drooped and needles dropped, yet we didn't care. The ornaments we had designed and constructed ourselves from colored paper and scraps of old string. Oddly enough, all of the best ornaments contained none of our *red* paper.

Janice had hogged it all.

Yet no one had argued with her. The dread of spending Christmas vacation in the hospital, in traction with poor Mr. Joe Sutter, constantly served as a warning.

A visitor came to our party. It was Mrs. Spinnerford, the librarian lady from the Learning Free Library. I liked her a whole lot because whenever she came calling, she'd read us a story or two. Miss Kelly also liked her. That was easy to tell, as our teacher offered Mrs. Spinnerford the chair that was close to our stove.

Cracking open a book, Mrs. Spinnerford read us a Christmas story, about ghosts. Even though I felt a bit sleepy from last night's excursion up Mulligan's Road, I still enjoyed her exciting story about mean old Mr. Scrooge and a poor little boy, Tiny Tim.

As she read, I did happen to notice that Mrs. Spinnerford eyed Soup and me with a well-founded mistrust, perhaps based on one of our earlier trips to her library and a foraging into the adult section on pictorial human physiology.

I whispered to Soup. "Ya know," I asked him, "what I like best about a Christmas party?"

"I give up."

"There's no geography."

After the story about Tiny Tim, the librarian lady stayed for a spell because Miss Kelly announced that we had a present to give her. So we all stood up and sang "Joy to the World." To my surprise, Mrs. Spinnerford sang along too; and she knew all the words, even without looking at a songbook.

Today was a good day, I was thinking. But tomorrow would prove even better, because Soup and I had planned to tackle our shopping. I'd be purchasing my three gifts for Mama, Papa, and Aunt Carrie.

"Well," said Mrs. Spinnerford, "I don't guess I can stay much longer until I wear out my welcome. So I best get marching."

Before she left, we all thanked her for coming. Miss Kelly thanked her three or four times and wished her a Merry Christmas.

Miss Kelly, I was thinking, looked close to respectable for our party. Even though she was wearing her raggy gray sweater and old shoes, at least she'd removed the pencil from her hair. On her shoulder she had pinned a paper flower of bright pink, something that the younger children had pasted together. It was a real mess. Smiling, she turned her head to smell it, pretending it was a rose.

I wanted to buy Miss Kelly a present too, but there would be precious little money left over by tomorrow.

Our teacher had baked some cupcakes, with sugary icing, all pink, which she passed to each of us I enjoyed mine with rapturous enthusiasm to the very final crumb, which I retrieved from the floor.

"They're real good," we told her.

Just as we were porking down the last of our cupcake treats, Miss Boland burst through the door like a winter wind, to holler us all a brief howdy-do.

"I can't stay or tarry," she told Miss Kelly.

"Why not?"

"Well, there's just too much decorating that needs my constant supervising. Most important," said Miss Boland, "is that I trot downtown pronto and instruct Harold Spencer how to untangle all those pesky strings of electrical Christmas lights. Harold says he'd like to get his hands on whoever packed 'em away last January."

"As I recall," Miss Kelly told her, "*you* did."

Both ladies laughed.

"Before *you* came along," Miss Kelly said to her friend, "I wonder how any of us ever prepared a Christmas, or how the world managed to turn. But I do hope you'll linger long enough to help me open the bag of presents that you brought for the children."

"Sure will," said Miss Boland.

Using her special key, Miss Kelly unlocked the bottom drawer of her desk and withdrew the bag, handing it to Miss Boland. She gently shook the rustling bag and its hidden mystery.

"I wonder what's in here," said our nurse.

"Presents!" we yelled.

Opening the bag, with a sly expression on her face, Miss Boland extracted and counted a whole fistful of little candy peppermint canes. Twenty-eight in all. She gave one to every kid. "It's not really a present from me," Miss Boland admitted. "They're all from Louie Graziano. I'm glad I got just barely enough."

I looked at my candy cane.

Sure enough, the red-and-white confection was a courtesy from one of our local merchants. The wrapper read: SHOP AT GRAZIANO'S GROCERY AND SAVE. The other kids ate their peppermint candy right away, but I saved mine.

Miss Boland left, but not before reminding us all to show up at the village square on Christmas Eve, to see Santa Claus and the lighting of our giant spruce tree. She shot a secret wink to Soup and me.

It was time for us to leave too.

As usual, we bundled ourselves into our heavy woolen coats and footwear. On her knees, Miss Kelly struggled with a boot for one kid and a balky mitten for another. She even wiped one first-grader's runny nose. Then we lined up at the door, behind Janice Riker, who, to no one's surprise, had bullied her way to the head of the line, to wish Miss Kelly a Merry Christmas.

Inside my mitten, I felt my candy cane.

Maybe, I was thinking, I'd take it home to show my folks, professing to Mama that it wasn't quite as good as getting a BB gun, but almost.

Yet, as I was about to say good-bye to Miss Kelly, a deeper feeling seemed to replace my earlier intention. I was glad I was the last kid in line, so nobody'd catch my doing it.

"Good night, Robert."

"Good night, Miss Kelly," I told her. And then, yanking off a mitten with my teeth, I handed her my peppermint cane. "Here," I said, "it's for you."

"Oh, thank you. But you mustn't give me *your* candy."

"Please take it," I said. "Because *we* all got one and you didn't. And because . . ."

Miss Kelly touched my face. "I know," she said softly. "Because I feel the same way about all of you. But perhaps you might think of something even better to do with your Christmas candy—if you remember the story we heard, about Tiny Tim."

I smiled up at her.

She nodded. "And thank you."

Soup had gone on ahead, so I started to run in order to catch up to Norma Jean Bissell, to give *her* my peppermint cane. She was walking with two other girls. But then I spotted Ally Tidwell, walking alone, like he always did, toward the railroad tracks and home.

"Tiny Tim," I heard myself saying.

I looked at Norma Jean, then at Ally, unable to decide quite what to do. Glancing back at Miss Kelly's school, I recalled what she'd told me. Then

I knew. So I ran to overtake Ally, because I didn't want him to be Tiny Tim, not at all.

"Here," I said, handing him my cane. "Candy's got a way of making me sick sometimes."

Ally stared at me. "Honest?"

"Yup, it turns me inside out. Same thing with Mama and Aunt Carrie, so I don't guess I can unload it on them. It'd be a shame to throw it away. Hey! Maybe you could give it to *your* mom, because peppermint goes so good with cheese."

He took it. "Thanks. Thanks a lot, Rob."

"Shucks," I said, "it's really from Mr. Graziano. He'll probable be at the tree lighting at the village square. So be sure to come yourself, and help us thank him personal. Will ya come?"

Ally nodded. "Okay."

"Good. Both Soup and I are coming for sure. We'll look for ya."

I was about to leave him, and take off to search for Soup or Norma Jean, but a sudden idea changed my idea. Right now, I had something more worthwhile to enjoy, so I did it.

I walked home with Ally.

10

Christmas Eve had almost arrived.

The white shawl of winter now covered Vermont's hardy shoulders, bringing with it the seasonal duties of shopping, shoveling, baking, wrapping, tree trimming, and defying pneumonia.

Soup's mother, Mama, and Aunt Carrie had peppered both of us with countless doses of cough syrup, Mother Gray's croup tablets, nasal sprays, and gargles. Now, and for many long winter weeks to follow, Soup's chest and mine would reek of Vicks VapoRub, mustard plaster, and goose grease. Plus a bag of camphor, which hung from each of our necks on a string.

Had even the most sturdy of germs come near me, it would have either screamed or perished. For twenty-four hours a day, my one unclogged nostril was forced to inhale fumes that could gag a maggot.

"Well," said Soup, "I hope the tree's ready for tonight."

"Yup," I said, "me too."

The two of us were standing in town, near the Double Zoomer, observing how Miss Boland was supervising the decorating activities of at least a dozen men. She was also quite busy herself, tinseling a park bench here, a lamppost there. She had even garlanded a fire hydrant.

"It's dangerous to stand still around here," one of her helpers muttered to another in a low voice. "If'n ya do, that Boland woman'll decorate ya."

Nearby, several of the electrical wizards of Learning were attempting to drape lengths of colored lights on the giant spruce tree. Needless to say, Miss Boland was directing the precise placement of every loop on every bow.

"Higher," she was hollering, "and to the left."

Two of the electricians were commenting on the

endless number of colored lights to be used. They also remarked on how our town of Learning would have to borrow plenty of added booster voltage from our neighboring villages, and that somebody had best inform Jason Willowby at the power plant.

"We'll need all the electrical juice we can splice to the main circuit," someone remarked.

Miss Boland continued to bark suggestions. "Harold, see if you can work it so the lights all twinkle. You know, on and off and on and off. Twinkling lights make a tree look prettier."

"But these ain't the twinkle kind," someone answered.

"No," she hollered up to Harold Spencer, who was forty feet up, atop an apple ladder. "You've got two green bulbs together, side by side."

"Nobody'll notice," Harold yelled down. "I'm above the clouds."

"There's two orange ones just within your reach." Miss Boland pointed. "Unscrew one, and swap it with a green. Or with a pink that's below your right boot. Maybe if you switch enough bulbs, they'll all *twinkle*."

"How come," Harold hollered back, "you wasn't so dagburn fussy when we had all of them lights away down yonder *on the ground?*"

Miss Boland pretended not to hear. As she turned away from the tree, spotting Soup and me, she came bustling our way.

"Boys," she said, "now you'll make sure Slosh Dubinsky gets here to the village square on time, in his Santa suit. He's to make his grand entrance right after we light up the tree."

We promised we'd see to it.

She nodded. "Good." Then, turning back to the big spruce tree, she shouted up at Mr. Spencer again. "No, Harold, one of the loops appears to be crooked. You might have to shinny up and balance yourself on the top rung to reach it."

"Not me," Harold told her, teetering atop his perch of peril. "I ain't much, but I'm all I got."

Soup and I watched for another minute.

"Rob," said Soup, "one more store."

"And we're done with shopping," I said. "Our folks will really be pleased with this stuff they're getting."

He was carrying his purchases, while I toted mine. Inside my bags nestled a box of mothballs, a bottle of laxative pills, and a rattrap. In Soup's, a pair of shiny-silver Shirly Temple shoe taps plus a plastic skull-head gearshift handle.

The two of us had splurged away every cent of our snow-shoveling currency, yet saved the most enticing establishment for our final stop.

Harry's Hardware Store.

Looking at the front window, however, both of us almost screamed in panic. There was no BB gun! But my apprehensions were quickly relieved as we burst into the store, for there it was, gleaming, shining, waiting for a kid named Rob Peck to become its devoted owner. Yanking off a mitten, I extended an exploratory hand. At last! I'd finally touched an Official Buck Jones Daisy Repeater BB Gun.

Neither Soup nor I had come to Harry's to trade. Only to spy, to see if the gun was still there, and perhaps to shield its visibility from other patrons.

"It's still here," I said.

"The very last one in town," said Soup.

High above the BB gun display stood an almost life-size cardboard likeness of the hero himself, Mr. Buck Jones, the bravest and truest cowboy to ride the celluloid ranges of Hollywood's movie mesa. And *this* was the same BB gun Buck used on Indians, grizzly bears, or tin cans.

Smack beside Buck's smiling western face was printed his personal message: "Little pardners, no mean ol' cattle rustler ever stands a chicken's chance when he's trapped in the sights of my trusty Official Buck Jones Daisy Repeater."

I didn't have to read Buck's quotation. His words I knew by heart, like a vesper.

"Soup," I asked, "do you actual suppose that one of us will really get this gun for Christmas?"

No answer.

Turning around, I noticed that Soup was gone. But then I spotted him in a nearby aisle, busily convincing a young customer that what he really wanted for Christmas was a football, *not* a BB gun. Good old Soup.

Mr. Harry Hoblicker, owner and proprietor of Harry's Hardware Store, had really gone all-out this Christmas. Red and green paper streamers looped and twisted across the leak-stained ceiling above Buck's cardboard grin. The cracked-plaster walls were festooned with silvery spangles, and golden balls dangled everywhere.

A big voice boomed behind me. "Luther? Is that you, Luther?"

Turning, I looked back and saw knees, then up, up, up, to see a white-bearded face. It was none other than our secret Santa for tonight, Mr. Slosh Dubinsky. Nobody seemed to want to stand near him. Eyes widening in sheer panic, they quickly scurried away.

"Hello," I finally chirped. If anything went afoul tonight, I was grateful he thought my name was Luther.

Bending down slowly, Mr. Dubinsky's face now closed in on mine. "Say," he said, "I ain't got no family, or nobody." Then he pointed a large finger at Buck Jones. "Do you reckon maybe a kid about your age would like to own a BB gun?"

My heart leaped!

"Wow," I told him, barely trusting myself to speak, "I sure would. I mean, *he* sure would."

Mr. Dubinsky smiled. "That's good," he told

me. "See ya tonight. Come to the pool parlor and tell me what I gotta do. Okay? Now run along and be a good boy, ya hear?"

I ran along.

But I sure didn't tell all of this to Soup. Even though I was itching to brag it out. Looking back, however, I couldn't see Mr. Dubinsky. The store was too crowded and I was too short. Yet I certain did see something else.

A farmer and his wife approached Buck Jones to examine the BB gun, checked the price tag, then moved toward me. The woman shook her head, muttering something about the Depression, a term I had begun to realize meant that hard times had hit town. Our local paper mill, I'd heard Papa say, was only running one day a week.

Although penniless, I still felt happy.

Somewhere above me, Mr. Hoblicker's loudspeaker was playing "Joy to the World." In school, for the past several weeks, Miss Kelly had taught us to sing it. My mind could picture our teacher directing us in her raggy gray sweater. To be honest, I liked singing "Joy to the World" even better than "Santa's On His Way to Town," but I couldn't explain exactly why.

Observing the milling mass of shoppers gave me another merry feeling. Because it sudden hit me what all of them were doing. Each person was hunting for a gift for somebody he loved. Somebody special. And that made everybody in the store special, too, like they were all Christmas angels.

As I looked at the people, I hoped I'd grow up to be like Mr. Graziano, our grocer, so I could give peppermint candy canes to everybody in the whole world. And then I'd share some of my groceries with people like the Tidwells.

Earlier, I'd sort of wanted to buy a present to give Soup, but we'd agreed, due to our limited resources, that we wouldn't give each other a gift. Our party at school, we figured, would be enough.

After all, if Soup and I were going to grow up and be regular Vermonters, the time was ripe to savor frugality. Cavalier spending hardly ran amuck in the Yankee genes of Pecks or Vinsons.

Looking around for Soup, I saw a whale of a lot of merchandise that I didn't want, even if we Pecks could have afforded it all. What I really wanted was to give stuff to people, even strangers. My arms were still holding the three presents for my family. Tonight, after chores and supper, I'd sneak upstairs and wrap each one real pretty. And tie bows.

"Joy to the World" crackled on and on.

It gave me the urge to walk among the people and share what little I had with everyone. "Here ya go, mister," I'd say. "Here's a pill for ya. And for you, lady, here's a mothball."

As I passed by the big cardboard Buck Jones, something was missing. I smiled, knowing why. The BB gun was gone. Then a brutal truth hit the pit of my stomach harder than a baseball bat. For sure, I sudden feared, Mr. Slosh Dubinsky had bought the gun I wanted.

For a kid he thought was *Luther!*

In other words—for Soup.

11

"Rob, here goes," said Soup.

Christmas Eve had finally arived. The two of us stood in front of Slosh's Hot-Time Pool Parlor, looked at each other, and snickered.

Other than Miss Boland, Soup and I were the only ones in Learning who knew the amusing fact that Santa Claus would be played this evening by the man with the meanest reputation in town, Mr. Stanley Dubinsky, locally known as Slosh.

We knocked.

The door opened, and the monster himself looked down at us. Slosh filled the entire entrance. He was carrying an enormous sack of stuff.

"Ho," he boomed. "Well, I'm ready. Where do I change into my Santa Claus costume?"

Soup swallowed. "Up north of here. Your Santa outfit is out Mulligan's Road, right near Mr. Joe Sutter's place."

Mr. Dubinsky blinked. "Mulligan's Road?"

Soup nodded. I noticed that my pal had somehow failed to mention his mysterious machine, or whatever it was Soup intended to assemble from the stuff in Mr. Sutter's barn.

"Okay," sighed Slosh. "How do we get there?"

"Don't you have a car?" I asked in a timid voice.

Mr. Dubinsky shook his head. "No thanks. I wouldn't own one. Because I never liked riding in them @#*$% things. Going fast makes me nervous. And I turn ornery. Them gas fumes make me sick."

Soup forced a smile. "Fine. We'll hoof it. But we really have to hurry some, or we'll be late for the tree lighting."

It was a long hike from the center of town all the way north, along the lake, to the very end of Mulligan's Road. The evening was cold, the north wind was blowing hard and into our faces, but we kept going. Not having too much time, at first we ran, then trotted, and finally walked. By the time we reached Mr. Sutter's, Soup and I, little as we were, were almost carrying poor old Mr. Dubinsky. He still, however, hung on tightly to his sack.

I wondered what was inside the sack, but was too afraid to ask its puffing owner.

"How—much—farther?" he wheezed.

"We're here," I told him.

"Thank—Heaven." Mr. Slosh Dubinsky collapsed into a heap against the high snowbank beside the road. "I—ain't—young—no—more."

"We can't rest *now*, Mr. Dubinsky," said Soup, "or we'll be late arriving at the tree."

Slosh rolled his eyes. "Oh, *no*," he panted weakly, "we gotta gallop all the way *back?*"

Soup gave his big shoulder a gentle pat. "Don't worry, sir. We got a surprise for ya. You won't have to walk hardly a step. In fact, you'll be riding in style."

Mr. Dubinsky's eyes widened, a look of genuine fright. "Riding? Riding in *what?*"

Soup smiled. "In your Santa Claus sleigh. Or rather, in Mr. Sutter's. But don't worry, there won't be any stinky old engine, no gasoline fumes to make you sick. And, as you know, a sleigh goes very slowly."

"Good," said Mr. Dubinsky. Gradually he regained his feet, shouldered his bulging sack, and even smiled. "Gee," he said, "it's gonna be fun, being Santa Claus."

"Let's go," I told him. We headed for the barn.

Mr. Joe Sutter is a very large man. But I had to admit, as Soup and I were stuffing, pushing, and shoehorning our new Santa into Joe's red Santa suit, that Slosh was even a size larger. How we did it I will never know. Yet our final result was one magnificent Santa Claus with real white whiskers all his own.

"How do I look?" he asked.

"Well," I told him, "you're the biggest Santa Claus that this town will ever get to enjoy."

"Thanks, Luther," he told me. "Both you boys are okay. I'm a lucky guy to be Santa." He smiled. "Well, now all I do is ride this here little sleigh into town. Right?"

"Right," said Soup.

Mr. Dubinsky looked confused. "Where's the *horses?*"

"We have another plan," Soup explained. "All we've got to do now is push the sleigh, plus our equipment, out of the barn and over to the lake. It's right nearby."

Slosh stared at the mass of assorted junk that Soup had piled into the sleigh. "What in @#$% is all this @#$% stuff?"

Soup grinned. "Uh, it's going to be your Christmas present. But it's sort of a surprise. You won't guess what it really is until we push the sleigh over to the ice. So please help."

As the barn door was open, plenty of snow had whirled inside, easing our job. The three of us, with mighty Mr. Dubinsky supplying most of the muscle, moved the little red sleigh out of the barn, closed the door, then pushed it over the crusty snow and onto the ice of the frozen lake. The front of the sleigh pointed south, toward Learning. The moonlight made the ice appear to be shiny and slick, polished by a fierce north wind.

"Now what?" asked Mr. Dubinsky. "There ain't no horses here. I don't see no @#$% horses."

At this point, I was as confused as Slosh. He didn't know Luther Wesley Vinson as well as I did. Soup, with his demon of a brain, had cooked up some crazy idea, which I now prayed would work.

Meanwhile, Soup wasn't idle. Item by item, he yanked all of his strange equipment, mostly junk, from the sleigh. It lay in a heap on the ice.

"I still don't get it," said Slosh, who was holding his large sack with one hand and the red Santa hat on his head with the other. The wind was really blowing.

Soup pointed to the sleigh. "Please climb aboard, Mr. Dubinsky, because we're almost ready to head for town."

Giving my pal a doubting look, and still muttering about our lack of horsepower, Slosh mounted the sleigh and sat on the single seat, holding the mysterious sack on his lap.

"Help me, Rob," said Soup, grabbing a bean pole.

The two of us never worked faster. Following Soup's bewildering instructions, we wired two of the long bean poles to the front of the sleigh. They stuck straight up in the air. We tied ropes to the four corners of the great big horse blanket, and knotted our ropes around the base of the two poles. Then we added the set of sleigh bells. We braced the edges of the horse blanket with poles, rather like a frame around a picture. It lay flat on the ice in front of the sleigh.

"It's finished," Soup told me, passing several loose ends of rope up to Slosh.

"Great, but what *is* it?" Slosh wanted to know.

Soup proudly smiled. "A sail."

"For a @#$% *sleigh?*"

"Sure," said Soup in a confident voice that only the insane possess. "So jump in, Rob, because we're all riding to Learning in style. Santa's On His Way to Town," he sang.

Into the sleigh we jumped, taking what little seating was available, as Mr. Dubinsky and his sack occupied most of it. Only half of my bottom had a seat. The other half hung over the edge. Slosh sat wedged between us. He was so large that Soup was out of my sight.

"Okay," said Soup, "please pull on the ropes, Mr. Dubinsky."

He pulled.

Up, up, up rose the pole-framed horse blanket, until it was vertical, high above our heads. At once it filled with air, and our little sleigh lurched forward, driven by a tenacious north wind.

100

"Hey," said Slosh, "it really works."

The sleigh was creeping at a steady rate, heading south toward town. All is well, I thought, breathing a deep and relieving sigh.

"But how do we steer?" asked Slosh.

"Easy," said Soup. "We just sort of pull on either one rope or the other."

Our sleigh picked up speed.

"It's a cinch," said Soup. "We glide merrily along over the ice to Emerson's Boat Dock, right near the village square. They'll all hear us coming because of our sleigh bells."

I had to admit Soup was right. We were sailing a sleigh, faster now, and our jingling bells seemed to be happier than we were. As our sleigh reached the widest and windiest part of the lake, our speed increased.

"We're going a bit rapid," said Mr. Dubinsky, tightening his grip on the ropes he was holding.

We were. Mr. Dubinsky was right. Our sleigh seemed to be gaining speed at a rather incredible rate.

"I don't like to ride fast," he said. "Inside, I'm really kind of a gentle person, and I don't like riding fast."

"Rob," I heard Soup say, "maybe there's a brake handle on your side. If there is, try pulling it back."

Carefully hooking an arm around one of Mr. Dubinsky's, I looked over the edge, seeing nothing but the blur of gray ice as it sped below. "There's no brake *here*," I told Soup. "Maybe it's on your side."

Soup apparently looked too. "Nope, it's not on this side either."

"No brake?" asked Mr. Dubinsky in the tiniest little Kewpie-doll voice I've ever heard.

"Don't worry," said Soup.

"I gotta jump off this @#*$% thing," wailed Mr. Dubinsky. As he started to rise from his seat, a sudden gust of north wind, from the rear, doubled our speed and kept Mr. Dubinsky seated. He fell back with a thundering thud.

Ahead of us, the amber lights of Learning, Vermont, were aglow, and appeared to be racing toward us, growing bigger and brighter every second. I could see that, luckily, we were headed more or less in the proper direction, toward Emerson's Boat Dock.

Faster and faster we streaked. Below us, I heard the steel runners hiss along the ice. The hissing grew louder and louder. So did our sleigh bells.

"We're out of control," yelped Mr. Dubinsky.

"Steer," hollered Soup. "All we gotta do is pull on the ropes, and we glide into town, off the lake, and into all that soft snow at the village square."

"No," said Mr. Dubinsky. "What we gotta do is take down that @#*$% horse blanket."

In a fury, he yanked on one of Soup's rotten old ropes. It snapped! Looking up, I saw that our top crossbar had somehow caught on the tips of the two upright poles, the points of which were now snagged into the fabric of the blanket.

"Lean," yelled Soup. "So we can stop the sleigh in that soft incline of snow, and coast to a stop."

"We're gonna crash," Mr. Dubinsky was screaming. "And I don't like to ride so fast. It's scaring the @#$% out of me."

"Don't worry," said Soup. "When people crash, they always stop."

"Lean," I yelled.

We leaned. It didn't help. Our speed had now surpassed a hundred miles an hour, and was closing in on two hundred. Ahead of us was *not* the soft incline of snow. Nor was it the boat dock.

Through my wind-whipped and watering eyes, I now saw where we were heading.

Straight for the Double Zoomer.

I prayed.

Soup hollered, "No. *No.* NO!"

Mr. Dubinsky grabbed us both, and swore.

Ahead, the gigantic Christmas tree was towering high above the Double Zoomer. All its festive lights suddenly burst into assorted colors, an illuminating tribute to Christmas, the electric genius of Mr. Harold Spencer, and borrowed voltage from our neighboring communities.

The steel runners on our sleigh now hissed like cobras as a choir of distant voices placidly sang "Santa's On His Way to Town."

Little did they know how soon.

Several things happened within the next five seconds: A sudden and powerful gust of north wind doubled our speed, snapped both upright poles, and blew away our horse blanket. Mr. Dubinsky said a dirty word. Soup and I ducked lower. And, worst of all, the curly runners of our sleigh entered the bottom of the Double Zoomer ice slide.

Never before, neither in fact nor legend, had anyone ever slid *up* the Double Zoomer. We had always slid *down*. But now, up we all climbed, as Santa hung on to Soup and me.

Up, up up . . .

As though the ice of windswept Lake Champlain had not been slick enough, the twin foot-polished ice tracks seemed to be slicker, smoother, and faster. Yet our sleigh scooted up the Double Zoomer, it seemed, for less than a second.

Then it reached the top of the icy slide. And, like a ski jumper, it took off. Up into the air.

When I was very young, I'd always believed that Santa Claus came to town on Christmas Eve flying through the skies on a sleigh. Now it was really happening. But without a ho-ho-ho from Mr. Dubinsky. Not even a cuss. He issued only one soft little moan of terror. Below, the open-mouthed faces of startled citizens looked up at us, with un-Christmasy disbelief.

But we made believers of them all.

Over their amazed expressions we soared; heading, as I now realized with terror, toward disaster.

Dead ahead stood the lighted Christmas tree. Bug-eyed, I watched the spruce tree growing as we flew toward it. Bigger . . . taller . . . wider . . .

CRASH! BAM! BOOM!

Just as our sleigh hit the Christmas tree, I heard the second loudest electrical explosion that anyone, anywhere, had ever heard. Sparks popped as lights shattered and electric cords encircled us. Followed by an even louder explosion, which blew out every light in Learning, in northern Vermont, in half of New Hampshire, and in several hamlets of Canada.

Adults screeched, but kids cheered.

It wasn't merely Christmas Eve. It was a mad combination of the Fourth of July, April Fool's Day, and Halloween, producing the most colorful display of bursting fireworks the wide-eyed citizenry of Learning had ever witnessed.

Down we sifted. Through the prickly spruce branches and sputtering sparks we tumbled—Santa and Soup and me. How we managed to avoid electrocution or a broken neck, I'll never be able to explain.

In a daze, Soup and I struggled to our feet, and helped Mr. Dubinsky. He also survived, having landed on Janice Riker, a fact that helped to make my Christmas Eve a lot merrier and safer.

Somebody pointed. "Look up yonder!"

I looked. A miracle was happening. The lights came *on* again, all over the tree! High in the spruce hung its only Christmas ornament, Mr. Joe Sutter's sleigh, caught between two enormous smoldering branches.

I noticed something else. For some reason, half of the Christmas tree lights were now twinkling. On, off, on, off. The other half merely continued to either emit sparks or explode.

"Ah," said Miss Boland, "they're *twinkling* at last."

"In case you ain't noticed," snorted Harold Spencer, "so's every doggone houselight in town."

It was true. Every light in Learning had become a twinkler.

No one seemed to care. Everyone was singing "Joy to the World," with the possible exception of Janice. Having someone the size of Slosh land on you rarely produces either joy or music. I noticed that Mr. Stanley Dubinsky, still in his slightly torn Santa suit, sang the loudest of all.

No sooner had the Christmas carol ended than someone pointed at Joe Sutter's sleigh again and then at Santa. "Hey, " he said, "it ain't Joe. It's *Slosh!*"

The entire crowd stilled to a deathly silence. Mouths fell open. Eyes stared in utter disbelief.

"Ho-ho-ho," Mr. Dubinsky laughed.

Without another word, he located his enormous pack, opened it, and passed out presents to people. Mostly to the youngsters. As he did it, the startled expressions on faces began to soften into friendly smiles. Folks even patted Slosh on the back, and best of all, the only name they called him was *Santa*.

Boys hugged him, and little girls gave him kisses.

It was then that I saw something that made me hold my breath. Reaching into his sack, Slosh extracted one very particular gift. It was an Official Buck Jones Daisy Repeater BB Gun.

"No," I said.

Worst of all, I knew that Mr. Dubinsky was about to call out the name *Luther*, and Soup would get my gun. My heart sank. All my hopes for Christmas were about to slip painfully away. Soup would own the BB gun, and I wouldn't. Pangs of envy went surging through my loins.

High above his head, Mr. Slosh Dubinsky held the one coveted prize. I saw Soup's face begin to smile. Darn him, he knew he was getting it, I was thinking.

"This gift," said Slosh, "is for a real special kid, because he's a good boy and helps his mother. He's earned it proper."

I waited, hurting all over.

"A Buck Jones BB Gun," said Slosh, "for Ally Tidwell."

I saw a grin on Ally Tidwell's face, and Soup gave me a nudge.

"I'm glad, Rob. I can't believe it, but I'm actual glad."

To my surprise, I felt even gladder. Maybe, I

thought, it was about time Ally got a hunk of happiness. And now he'd believe in Christmas forever. Not because he got a BB gun. But because Santa had said he'd *earned it.* I felt gladdest when I noticed that Ally's mother, Mrs. Tidwell, had come too.

"And that ain't all," Mr. Dubinsky went on to say as he handed the gun to a beaming Ally Tidwell. "From now on, every kid in this here town can call me—Uncle Stanley."

The entire crowd was smiling.

"But," warned Slosh, "them slobs at the pool parlor better not call me Uncle Stanley, unless they want to git stood on their heads."

Everybody laughed.

An hour later, five of us were thawing ourselves out in the cozy warmth of Miss Kelly's kitchen. She had invited Miss Boland, Mr. Dubinsky, Soup, and me for a tasty mug of hot cocoa. Every minute or so, her houselights would twinkle, and we would all laugh like crazy.

Mr. Dubinsky was still wearing the Santa suit. He looked very tired, yet very pleased.

"My," said Miss Kelly, "what an evening. I shall never again see so wonderful a Santa Claus make such a dramatic arrival."

"And," said Miss Boland, "the town certainly can't blame it *all* on me." She looked at Soup and me, then chuckled.

"Maybe," said Slosh, "I didn't make so good a

110

Santa." His face fell. "I sort of crashed into Christmas."

Miss Kelly touched his hand. "Stanley," she said to Slosh, "ever since you and I attended school together, years ago, I always suspected that there was a secret Santa somewhere inside you."

"Likewise," said Miss Boland. "And I'm powerful happy that you final showed your good side to the whole doggone population. Best of all, you let yourself enjoy it. Stanley, in more ways than one, you made the whole town twinkle."

Mr. Dubinsky held up a protesting paw. "Hold it now, ladies," said Slosh. "I'm the guy who operates the Hot-Time Pool Parlor. So I can't honest pretend to be no little *angel*."

Blowing the sudsy head off his cocoa, Slosh took another sip.

Miss Kelly smiled. "An angel," she said softly, "is not always small or in a white robe or with long golden hair. Angels come in all sizes and guises. And when our hearts know that we have our very own *special angel,* I guess it makes us the richest folks on earth."

I looked up at my three grown-up friends. We had *three* angels, I thought, not just one.

"Gee," said Slosh, "I'm an angel." He grinned. "Maybe the guys at the pool parlor will kid me about this. But I'll just shrug it off."

Seeing as it was getting late, and because Christmas morning brings farm chores before other activities, it was time for Soup and me to leave. Our big Santa, a nurse, and a teacher all hugged us and pointed us for home.

Walking uproad, neither Soup nor I talked too much. Hardly at all. I was listening to the squeaky music our boots created on the road's hard-packed snow.

Above us, the December sky was clear and quiet. Stars were blinking. One star looked brighter, and I wanted to touch it, because that one special star made me feel that getting a Buck Jones BB Gun wasn't so important. Already I'd been given more joy than my heart could hold. And I had me a hunch that my best pal, Soup, was feeling equal as merry.

We didn't even have to whistle. Our silent night of Christmas Eve was singing it all.

SOUP
RIDES AGAIN!

Whether he's riding into trouble on horseback or rolling into trouble on an outrageous set of wheels, Soup and his best friend Rob have a knack for the kind of crazy mix-ups that are guaranteed to make you laugh out loud!

☐ SOUP 48186-4 $2.95

☐ SOUP AND ME 48187-2 $2.95

☐ SOUP FOR PRESIDENT 48188-0 $2.50

☐ SOUP IN THE SADDLE 40032-5 $2.75

☐ SOUP ON FIRE 40193-3 $2.95

☐ SOUP ON ICE 40115-1 $2.75

☐ SOUP ON WHEELS 48190-2 $2.95

☐ SOUP'S DRUM 40003-1 $2.95

☐ SOUP'S GOAT 40130-5 $2.75

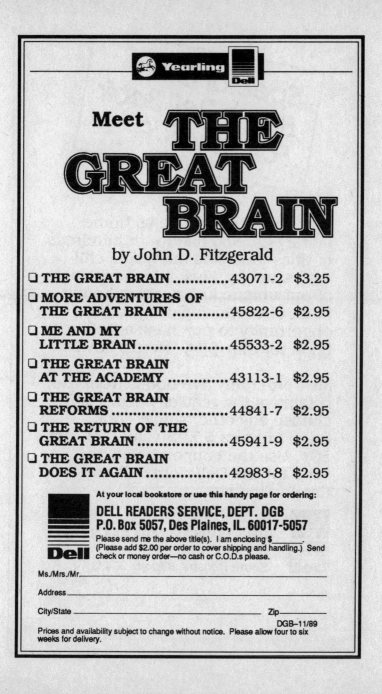

Special Offer
Buy a Dell Book
For only 50¢.

Now you can have Dell's Home
Library Catalog filled with hundreds
of titles including many fine children's books. Plus, take advantage
of our unique and exciting bonus
book offer which gives you the
opportunity to purchase a Dell
book for only 50¢. Here's how!

Just order any five books from the
catalog at the regular price. Then
choose any other single book
listed (up to a $5.95 value) for just
50¢. Use the coupon below to
send for the Dell Home Library
Catalog today.

DELL HOME LIBRARY CATALOG
P.O. Box 1045
South Holland, Illinois 60473

Ms./Mrs./Mr._____

Address _____

City/State _____ Zip _____